from the guttering.
Sometimes seen causing
mischief and mayhem
before scampering away
over rooftops.

Read all the Gargoylz adventures!

Gargoylz on the Loose!

Gargoylz Get Up to Mischief

Gargoylz at a Midnight Feast

Gargoylz Take a Trip

Gargoylz Put On a Show

Gargoylz

Put On a Show

Burchett & Vogler
illustrated by Leighton Noyes

RED FOX

GARGOYLZ PUT ON A SHOW
A RED FOX BOOK 978 1 849 41033 5

First published in Great Britain by Red Fox,
an imprint of Random House Children's Books
A Random House Group Company

This edition published 2009

1 3 5 7 9 10 8 6 4 2

Series created and developed by Amber Caravéo

The Random House Group Limited supports the Forest Stewardship
Council (FSC), the leading international forest certification organization.
All our titles that are printed on Greenpeace-approved FSC-certified paper
carry the FSC logo. Our paper procurement policy can be found at
www.rbooks.co.uk/environment

Set in Bembo Schoolbook

Red Fox Books are published by Random House Children's Books,
61–63 Uxbridge Road, London W5 5SA

www.**kids**a**trandomhouse**.co.uk
www.**rbooks**.co.uk

Addresses for companies within The Random House Group Limited can be
found at: www.randomhouse.co.uk/offices.htm

THE RANDOM HOUSE GROUP Limited Reg. No. 954009

A CIP catalogue record for this book is available from the British Library.

Printed and bound in Great Britain by CPI Bookmarque, Croydon, CR0 4TD

For Katie Burchett who is going to fulfil her dream
without the help of a wolf suit

- Burchett & Vogler

For my super cool little cousin Joshua Brimelow, with love

- Leighton Noyes

Hello, I'm the Web Gargoyle.
Look out for me – I'll be hiding in one
of the pictures in the book.
When you spot me, be sure to make a
note of the secret codeword I'm holding.
The codeword unlocks a secret level
of the amazing Gargoylz game
on our fabulous website at
www.gargoylz.co.uk

Oldacre Primary School

garden

staff car park

staffroom

playing field

playground

St Mark's Church

playground

a little mole in a hole

School Report - Max Black

Days absent: 0

Days late: 0

Max is never afraid to make a contribution to history lessons. His demonstration of a battering ram using a broom and a bucket was very realistic, although the resulting hole in the classroom door was not ideal.

I worry that Max only seems to play with Ben Neal, but he assures me he has a lot of friends at the local church.

Class teacher - Miss Deirdre Bleet

Max Black's behaviour this term has been outrageous. He has repeatedly broken school rule number 739: boys must not tell 'knock knock' jokes in assembly. He is still playing pranks with Ben Neal. Mrs Pumpkin is absent again after the exploding paint pot incident. And Mrs Simmer, the head dinner lady, says the mincing machine has never been the same since he fed his maths test into it.

Head teacher - Hagatha Hogsbottom (Mrs)

School Report - Ben Neal

Days absent: 0

Days late: 0

This term Ben has
been very inventive in PE.
However, attempting to tightrope-walk
across the hall was a little dangerous
- and used up all the skipping ropes.
He spends far too much time in class
looking out of the window and waving at
the gravestones in the churchyard. He
would be better learning his spellings - a
word he insists on writing as 'spellingz'.

Class teacher - Miss Deirdre Bleet

Ben Neal is always polite, but I am deeply concerned
about his rucksack. It often looks very full - and
not with school books, I am certain. It has sometimes
been seen to wriggle and squirm. I suspect that he
is keeping a pet in there. If so, it is outrageous and
there will be trouble.

Head teacher - Hagatha Hogsbottom (Mrs)

Contents

1. The Play's the Thing   1

2. Costume Chaos   33

3. Who's Afraid of the Big Bad Wolf?   61

4. Show Time!   85

1. The Play's the Thing

Max Black and Ben Neal mooched down the road towards Oldacre Primary School. For once they weren't zooming along in one of their imaginary spy vehicles. They were too fed up.

"Monday morning assembly," groaned Max. "I don't think we'll survive."

"Thirty minutes of nagging and moaning by Mrs Hogsbottom, the scariest head teacher in the world," agreed Ben.

Max grabbed his arm. "It could be even worse. Lucinda Tellingly might be singing like last Monday!"

1

Ben shuddered. "We need a plan –
Secret Plan: Assembly Escape," he decided.

Just as they reached the school gates,
the bell rang. The playground bustled with
children swarming into class.

"I wish we could find the gargoylz and play some tricks," sighed Max, ignoring the bell. "That would take our minds off assembly."

Max and Ben had some very unusual friends. The gargoylz were stone creatures that lived on the church beside the school. Each one had a special power, and there was nothing they enjoyed more than making mischief. The two boys were the only humans who knew the gargoylz could come to life.

Max ran across to the playground wall and craned his neck over to check the church gutters. Their friends sometimes hung there, keeping perfectly still in case anyone was watching.

"Any sign of them?" asked Ben, squeezing behind a bush to join him.

"Max Black and Ben Neal!" boomed a voice.

Codename:
Evil Head
Teacher

SPY FILE:

Max activated his spy radar: grey hair, beaky nose, face like a sour lemon. He knew what that meant. It was Enemy Agent Mrs Hogsbottom, commonly known as Mrs Hogsbum, codename: Evil Head Teacher.

She was leaning out of her office window and glaring at them. "School rule number seventy-nine," she bellowed. "Boys must not hide in bushes and peer over playground walls. Get to your classroom at once."

Ben and Max headed gloomily for the door.

* * *

The boys sat with their class in the hall while the rest of the school trooped in.

"The seconds are ticking by, Agent Neal," muttered Max, "and we haven't worked out our Secret Plan: Assembly Escape."

"Too late," groaned Ben. "Here comes Mrs Hogsbum now. Get ready for the nagging."

But to their amazement, the head teacher was smiling. All the children looked a bit startled at this unusual sight.

"You'll be very excited about this," she announced. "As you know, Oldacre School puts on a play every year. And this year it's Year Four's turn to do it.

Anyone interested in taking part should see Miss True at playtime."

"That's us!" breathed Ben. "Awesome."

At lunch time the boys sped into the playground to tell their gargoyle friends the amazing news.

Making sure that Mrs Hogsbottom was nowhere in sight, they raced over to the churchyard wall.

"Greetingz!" A beaming, monkey-faced gargoyle landed next to them.

"Hi, Toby," said Max. "We've got great news."

"I must fetch the others!" Toby spread his wings and flew round the church roof, calling out to all the friends he could find.

Three eager gargoylz – Theo, Azzan and Barney – scampered over to the wall and waved to Max and Ben.

"The rest are at the pond in the park," explained Theo, a small stripy gargoyle who looked rather like a cat. "They're watching Ira chase the ducks like a fierce pirate."

"What's the news?" asked Azzan, swishing his dragony tail in excitement.

"School's going to be cool for a change," Ben told the gargoylz eagerly. "We're going to put on a play!"

"A play! A play! Hurray!" yelled a voice, and Zack appeared out of thin air. He charged along the wall and skidded to a halt, his shaggy-maned head on one side. "What's a play?"

"A play's when you act out a story for people to watch," explained Ben.

"And this one's the story of Red Riding Hood," added Max. "Miss True's going to be in charge and she's not too bad — for a teacher. She told us all about it at a special meeting at playtime."

"A story about a hood?" said Azzan, snorting a small jet of fire from his nose. Blasting out fire was his special power but he couldn't always control it. "Sounds boring."

"It's a fairy tale," Ben explained, "about a little girl who *wears* a red hood and goes to see her grandma with a basket of food . . ."

". . . but a fierce wolf has eaten her grandma," Max went on.

"Wolves don't eat grandmas," said Toby doubtfully.

9

"This one does," insisted Max. "Then he gets into bed and pretends to *be* Grandma."

"He'd never get away with it." Theo shook his head firmly. "Grandmas aren't furry."

"Anyway," said Max, wondering if he'd ever get to the end of the story, "Little Red Riding Hood fetches a woodcutter, who cuts open the wolf's tummy – and out comes Grandma, still alive! The wolf had swallowed her whole."

"Dangling drainpipes!" exclaimed Toby in amazement. "That wolf should learn to chew his food."

"Sounds like fun," declared Zack bouncing around eagerly.

"What are you boys going to be in the play?" asked Barney.

"I don't want a speaking part," Max told him. "It's too much work. The only trouble is, if I don't have a speaking part,

Miss True might make me be a singing tree or a dancing squirrel instead."

"I want to be the woodcutter," said Ben. "I can do some awesome chopping."

He lifted an imaginary axe and swung it down on the wall. Barney was so scared he let off one of his terrible smells. It was his special gargoyle power – but sometimes it happened accidentally.

"Time to go," said Ben, turning green and flapping a hand in front of his face. "You can all watch me practise tomorrow."

"Hurray!" chorused the gargoylz merrily.

"But no pretending to chop us up!" Barney called after the boys as they ran off to escape the stink.

At playtime the next morning the five
gargoylz lined up on the churchyard wall.

Then Barney hid behind Toby, the spines
on his back quivering as Ben sped towards
them, chopping at the air.

Max followed, flapping a piece of
paper. "I'm going to help Ben," he told
them. "He's trying to learn one of the
woodcutter's speeches from this script here.
Then he'll say it in front of Miss True to
see if he gets the part in the show. That's
called an audition."

"She'd better choose Ben," said Azzan,
"or I'll singe her socks."

"And I'll turn into a tiger," declared Theo boldly, "and scare her singed socks off!" Theo thought he was very scary, especially when he used his special power to turn into a tiger. But as he was a young gargoyle – just four hundred and twelve years old – he hadn't quite got the hang of being a tiger yet and could only turn himself into a cute, stripy kitten.

"Thanks," Ben said. "Let's start. Max, you be the wolf."

Ben leaped at Max, swishing his arms wildly over his head. "*Fee, fi, fo, fum!*" he cried.

"That's *Jack and the Beanstalk*," hissed Max.

"I mean, *Ah-ha, you nasty wolf*," Ben began again. "*You won't get away* . . . No, er . . . *You won't escape* . . . um . . ."

"*You've eaten your last grandma*," Max told him, checking the script, "*and you won't escape my trusty axe.*"

"*You've eaten your last grandpa,*" Ben
ploughed on. He swished the imaginary
axe through the air. "*Take that, you horrible,
er . . .*"

". . . *wolf,*" prompted Max.

"I wonder if I need a *tiny* bit more
practice," sighed Ben.

"Much more practice! Much more
practice!" said Zack cheerfully as Ben
went off to study the piece of paper.

"Zack's right," Toby said, looking gloomy. "At the moment Ben's not even good enough to be a singing tree!"

"I know," whispered Max, "and the auditions are after lunch. Ben's going to need some help if Miss True's going to choose him as the woodcutter."

The gargoylz nodded solemnly. At that moment the bell went.

"Don't worry," said Toby. "We'll come up with a super-duper, special secret plan to help Ben."

After lunch Ben rushed eagerly into the hall for his audition. Max hunted around

the playground in search of the gargoylz.
Ben had practised his lines
in between mouthfuls
of pasta but he was
still getting his
words wrong.
Max hoped the
gargoylz *had*
come up with
a really good
secret plan.

But he
couldn't find them
anywhere. Finally
he gave up and went
along to the hall to join Ben.
Mrs Hogsbottom and Miss True were
sitting in the front row; a group of Year
Four children were sitting behind them.

Making sure the teachers weren't
looking, Max crept up the steps and darted
off to the side of the stage.

There was a group of boys all waiting behind the open curtain to audition for parts in the show. Ben was in the middle.

"I might not know all my lines," he said cheerfully, "but my acting will be so good they won't notice."

"I hope you're right!" muttered Max desperately.

"Max Black!" came a voice. Max's spy radar whizzed into action: long blonde plait, Australian accent, keen as a kangaroo. He knew what that meant. It was Enemy Agent Miss True, codename: Not Too Bad for a Teacher. She was right behind him. "Are you auditioning for the woodcutter?"

SPY FILE:

Codename:
Not Too Bad
for a Teacher

"No!" said Max in horror. "I don't want a speaking part. But I don't want to be something sweet like a dancing tree or a squirrel either – or a toadstool or a signpost or a—" he added hurriedly.

"Hold your horses!" laughed Miss True. "We're starting with people who want to be the woodcutter. Take a seat and watch."

Max returned to the front of the stage and sidled into a seat with the rest of his class, as far away from the head teacher as he could get. There was nothing he could do to help his friend – and the gargoylz were nowhere to be seen. He stared miserably at the spotlit stage. There were various painted bushes and cardboard animals propped up at the back, left over from the last play.

"Who's first?" bellowed Mrs Hogsbottom.

Nigel, the smallest boy in the class, crept on and began. His knees knocked as he mumbled his way through his speech, but at least he knew his lines. This did not look good for Ben.

Suddenly a small tabby kitten appeared from the side of the stage and started weaving around Nigel's legs. Max's eyes lit up. This was no ordinary kitten. It was Theo in his 'ferocious tiger' form!

The gargoylz had
come to the rescue!
Nigel wobbled,
then tottered
backwards into a
paper bush.

Mrs Hogsbottom
shot to her feet,
steam coming
out of her ears.
"Outrageous!"
she bawled. "The
woodcutter doesn't have a
cat. Get rid of it at once. Next!"

Max leaped to his feet. This was his
chance to get back to Ben and see how he
was doing with his lines. "I'll catch Theo
– er – the kitten," he offered, jumping up
onto the stage and chasing the mischievous
little cat around the scenery.

"Brilliant plan, Theo!" he whispered as
he finally managed to scoop him up. "Get

rid of all the other woodcutters and Ben's sure to be given the part."

"Leave it to us," purred Theo happily. He jumped out of Max's arms and disappeared into the dark.

Max found Ben in the wings at the side of the stage, studying the words on his script.

"I just can't remember all this," he sighed, throwing it to the floor.

"Never fear, Agent Neal." Max tapped his nose. "Secret help is at hand!"

As he spoke, there was a **pop!** and Zack appeared out of thin air, snatched the script and vanished again. The paper bobbed off behind the curtain.

Max looked at Ben in alarm. But to his surprise his friend was grinning. "If the gargoylz have got a plan, everything will be all right," he said. "Who's next?"

Max turned to look at the stage and his spy radar picked up trouble: shaved head, big fists, eyes like a rattlesnake.

He knew what that meant. It was Enemy Agent Barry Price, also known as The Basher, codename: School Bully.

"It's Barry," Max told Ben, his eyes sparkling. "I can't wait to see what the gargoylz have got in store for him!"

The Basher shouted his lines and stomped about like a thunderstorm.

Max and Ben heard a mischievous

giggle from above and then a cascade
of pink glitter rained down on Barry,
covering him from head to foot.
He stood there, open-mouthed,
spluttering and sparkling in the
spotlights. The boys looked up
to see Toby and Azzan sitting
on a lighting rig with
an empty bucket.

They were both covered in glitter
as well. Max gave them a
thumbs-up. Toby winked
merrily and the two
gargoylz scurried away.

"That was the
magic fairy dust from
Peter Pan last year!"
exclaimed Ben.

"Barry looks like a
girl," Max whispered
in delight.

Gasping, The Basher
stormed off the stage, leaving
fairy-dust footprints behind him.

"School rule number three hundred
and ninety-six!" they heard Mrs
Hogsbottom yell. "Woodcutters must
not get covered in glitter. Next!"

"I'm on after The Basher," Ben said,
standing up. "It's my turn now." He strode
onto the stage and gave a deep bow.

"Hmmph!" grunted Mrs Hogsbottom disapprovingly.

Ben raised his imaginary axe and swished it a few times. "*Ah-ha!*" he began at full volume. "*You nasty red grandma. You've eaten your last wolf* . . . I mean . . . um . . ." He ground to a halt.

Max's heart sank to his trainers. Ben still didn't know his lines. Then he saw something among the spotlights above Ben's head. A small stone-coloured shape was swinging by its tail from a cardboard crescent moon and flapping Ben's script at him. Toby had come to help!

Ben squinted at the script. "*Ah-ha! You've beaten* . . . er, *eaten* . . . Hold still, I can't see what it says!"

The moon, hanging by a cord, had begun to twist. Toby spun round with it.

"*And you won't escape my trusty* . . ." Ben was craning his neck to try and read the revolving piece of paper. "I can't see," he muttered. "It's covered in glitter!"

Ben stumbled to the end of his speech. He lifted his imaginary axe and swung it through the air. "*Bake that, you worrible hoof!*" he yelled.

"Spluttering gutterz!" came Toby's admiring voice from above. "What a brilliant performance."

With a triumphant grin, Ben bowed to the audience and ran off stage.

Gavin Steele was next. As soon as he opened his mouth, the boys could see he was really good. His words rang out across the hall. And he had a real cardboard axe.

Ben's face fell. "The gargoylz had better get rid of him quickly!" he muttered.

Just then, Max spotted a stone nose peeping out of a sack of gold in the corner. It was Barney.

The little gargoyle's eyes glazed over and a terrible pong drifted onto the stage.

Gavin dropped his axe, his face went
purple and he began to gasp.

"That should do it!" declared Ben,
pulling his jumper up over his face to
escape the dreadful smell.

"He can't carry on now," agreed Max, holding his nose and trying not to explode with laughter.

But to the boys' amazement, Gavin picked up his axe and started to fan the air. He was flapping the smell away – towards the audience – and carrying on with his speech at the same time!

Mrs Hogsbottom and Miss True were sitting there, mesmerized by Gavin's excellent performance. Then Barney's bottom burp hit them.

"Everybody out!" shrieked the horrified head, shooing the rest of the audience towards the safety of the corridor. "And whoever did that will have no playtime for ten years!" As soon as the hall was empty, the four gargoylz popped up from behind the scenery. They rushed over to the boys.

"I haven't had so much fun since we retyped the vicar's sermon and made him say sausages on every line," chortled Toby.

"Ben's the best woodcutter ever!" declared Zack, bouncing up and down on the stage.

"It was an awesome plan, gargoylz," cried Max, high-fiving with Ben.

"The part's *got* to be mine now," Ben said happily. "After all, I was the only one who got to the end of my audition."

2. Costume Chaos

The next morning Max and Ben raced into the classroom on their imaginary superspy hover-jets. The moment lessons started, they would find out if Ben had got the part of the woodcutter.

"Listen, everyone!" came a weedy voice from the front of the class. Max's radar burst into action: short and dumpy, limp brown hair, feeble smile. He knew what that meant. It was Enemy Agent Miss Bleet, codename: Wimpy Teacher.

She was nervously flapping a piece of paper. "I have a list of the children chosen to be in the play," she declared.

The class began chattering excitedly.
Max and Ben crossed their fingers.

Miss Bleet tried to shout above the
noise. "Red Riding Hood will be played
by . . . Lucinda Tellingly."

Lucinda and her best friend, Tiffany,
hugged each other, and Lucinda looked
around at the rest of the class with a smug
smile.

"Yuck!" gasped Max and Ben together.

"Grandma," Miss Bleet ploughed on,
"will be Tiffany Goodchild."

Tiffany and
Lucinda squealed
and hugged
each other
again. Ben
pretended to
be sick.

"And the
woodcutter is . . ."

Ben sat absolutely
still. This was his big moment.

". . . Gavin Steele," announced Miss
Bleet.

Ben slumped miserably in his seat.

Miss Bleet carried on reading out the
other parts in the play. "Head squirrel –
Duncan . . . woodcutter's wife – Felicity . . ."

At last their teacher folded up the list.

"I didn't even get picked to be a
dancing tree," sighed Ben. "I can't believe
Miss True hasn't spotted my great talent."
He looked over to where the woodcutter

was being patted on the back by his friend and head squirrel, Duncan. "I would have been loads better than Gavin – once I'd learned my lines."

But Miss Bleet hadn't finished. "That just leaves Max and Ben," she said. "Miss True has a very special part lined up for you two."

"Bet it's woodland elves," groaned Ben.

"Or tap-dancing toads," added Max dismally.

"You two will play the part of – *the wolf*!" announced their teacher.

"The wolf!" shouted Ben, jumping up in excitement. "That's amazing!"

Max grinned too, but then he frowned. "I don't understand," he said to Miss Bleet. "We can't *both* be the wolf."

"You can," she explained, "because the wolf costume needs two people inside it, like a pantomime horse. Ben wanted a speaking part so he's going to be the front."

"Cool!" Ben whacked Max on the back and nearly knocked him off his chair.

"And Miss True said Max was so good at crawling about after that cat yesterday that he'll be a perfect wolf rear end," Miss Bleet finished.

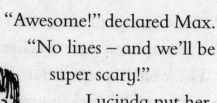

"Awesome!" declared Max. "No lines – and we'll be super scary!"

Lucinda put her hand up. "What about costumes?" she asked sweetly.

"The costumes are being delivered this afternoon by Bodkins, the costume shop in the village," Miss Bleet told the class. "They're kindly donating some old stock. Now, that's enough about the play. Time for maths."

But Max and Ben weren't listening.

"The wolf!" gasped Max. "It's a dream come true!"

"It's even cooler than being the woodcutter!" said Ben.

"We'll have razor-sharp claws!"

exclaimed Max.

"And fearsome teeth," added Ben.

"We'll chase Lucinda all over the
stage . . ." said Max.

". . . and gobble up Tiffany!" finished Ben in delight. "We'd better get practising straight away."

"We'll be the most menacing wolf in the history of menacing wolves," said Max, with a roar that made the girls cower in their seats.

"Max Black, you haven't
been listening," quavered Miss
Bleet. "What's two times ten?"

"Easy!" growled Max in his
best wolf voice. "Twenty-seven."

Miss Bleet sighed.

Max shrugged. "Wolves don't go to school," he explained.

The boys practised being the wolf in every lesson and right through playtime. They sent Harry, the class gerbil, scurrying for cover, ruined a football game, and terrified Miss Bleet so much that she had to sit in the corner and fan herself with a hankie. They even frightened The Basher by mistake and were forced to run away, pretending their growls were bad coughs.

"I've had enough of you two," said Miss Bleet after playtime,

when Lucinda complained that Max
and Ben had chased her around the
playground insisting she was their lunch.
"If you can't behave yourselves and read
your English books, you won't be the
wolf after all."

The boys looked
at each other in
disbelief.

"Disaster, Agent
Black!" whispered
Max. "Time for
Secret Plan: Be on
Best Behaviour."

"We've never
tried that before,
Agent Neal," said
Ben, looking worried.

"It won't be for long,"
Max assured him. "Once we've
got our costume, no one will dare take our
starring role away from us."

They sat bolt upright in their seats, reading their books like perfect pupils.

"I'm going to explode with boredom," muttered Ben after five minutes.

"We can do it," Max muttered back grimly. "Think of the fearsome wolf costume."

As he spoke, a cheery stone face pressed its nose against the window beside them.

"It's Toby," whispered Ben. "Ignore him."

"You're right," agreed Max. "We can't risk joining in with gargoyle tricks now."

Out of the corners of their eyes the boys could see their little friend sticking out his tongue and waggling his ears at them. Stifling their giggles, they buried their noses in their books.

Toby walked up and down the window ledge on his front paws. Then he puffed up his cheeks until he was red in the face and blew raspberries on the glass. Ben screwed his eyes tightly shut and Max stuffed his hankie in his mouth.

At last Toby gave up and flew off, looking cross. Max and Ben glanced at each other. They'd have a lot of explaining to do when they saw their friend later.

The next instant there was a **pop!** and Zack appeared in front of them. He looked at the boys' horrified faces and gave a cheery grin.

"I squeezed through the window," he said. "Toby sent me on a mission – to stop you two being boring! Here goes!"

Before the boys could speak he'd vanished into thin air again. Max gave a gasp and nudged Ben. Miss Bleet's chair was moving on its own – just as she was about to sit on it. Too late! Their shocked teacher landed on the floor with her feet in the air. Max rushed over to help her up. He could hear Zack chuckling in his ear.

Then Ben yelled and pointed at the gerbil cage. The door was opening on its own! Propping Miss Bleet up at her desk, Max threw himself across the room like a goalie, scattering books and pencils in his wake – but it was too late. Thanks to the invisible Zack, Harry was already scampering away across the floor.

Now the whole class was falling over each other and knocking tables aside as they tried to catch the runaway Harry. Max was in despair. How could he and Ben stop Zack from ruining their Be on Best Behaviour plan? He could see the

mischievous gargoyle perched on the computer, laughing and popping in and out of view.

"No more pranks, Zack!" Max hissed into the air. "It's important."

It was one of the hardest things he'd ever had to say in his life.

Lucinda took charge of the gerbil rescue mission. "Leave this to me!" she announced over the din. "I'm good with animals. Come to Lucy-wucy, Harry." She crawled under the tables making ghastly squeaking noises.

This was too much for Ben. "I saw him run up your leg," he hissed in her ear. Lucinda let out a deafening shriek and leaped around the room, arms flailing at her dress.

Meanwhile Max spotted Harry scampering towards the door. "Agent Black to the rescue!" he declared.

He pounced on the runaway gerbil and came up holding him firmly in his cupped hands. "Got him!" he shouted to the class. Everyone cheered – apart from Lucinda, who scowled.

While the class was busy tidying up under Miss Bleet's instructions, Ben grabbed Zack and pushed him firmly out of the window.

"Max and Ben are no fun today," he heard Zack telling Toby.

"Can't think why," came Toby's reply. "I haven't laughed so much since we rang the bellz at midnight and the vicar ran into church in his pyjamaz."

Ben turned to find Miss Bleet at the front of the class, clinging onto the whiteboard for support.

"Thank you, Max and Ben," she croaked. "For once you've been really kind and helpful."

The boys beamed.

"Almost as kind and helpful as Lucinda," their teacher went on, staggering over to her chair.

The boys' smiles froze in disgust. But before they could protest, the bell rang for lunch time.

"What an insult!" exclaimed Max as they trooped out into the playground. "She compared us with a girl!"

"Teachers have no idea how hurtful they can be," sighed Ben.

"There are the gargoylz!" exclaimed Max, waving at a line of stony shapes on the staffroom roof above them. "But they don't look too pleased to see us."

"Can't blame them," said Ben bitterly. "We've never spoiled their tricks before! I hope they still want to be our friends."

They gave the gargoylz a sheepish wave. The little creatures stared sternly back.

"What's going on?" demanded Toby, frowning down over the gutter.

"Very silly behaviour!" said Zack disapprovingly.

Theo, Barney and Azzan nodded solemnly in agreement.

"We're very sorry we couldn't join in with your tricks," said Max.

"And such mega-brilliant tricks too!" added Ben with a sigh.

Zack perked up at this. "Classroom chaos! Classroom chaos!" he chirped, bouncing on the spot.

"We had to stop you," Max told them. "The thing is – we're going to be the stars of the school play ..."

"... but we have to be good till the costume arrives ..." added Ben.

"... or we don't get the part," finished Max.

"Oh," said Toby, grinning. "In that case, we forgive you."

"What part is it?" asked Theo.

"Not the woodcutter?" Barney asked, looking disappointed.

"Better than that," said Ben, baring
his teeth and giving a growl. "We're going
to be the wolf!"

"We've got a costume that we'll both
fit in together and we're going to be super
scary," added Max. "With razor-sharp
claws."

"And fearsome teeth," growled Ben.

The gargoylz gave a cheer. Even
Barney grinned – from behind his paws.

"It's all right, Barney," Ben reassured
the trembling little gargoyle. "We won't be
eating *you*."

"So, you see, you mustn't make mischief before we get our costume," Max told them.

"No tricks?" asked Theo.

"*No!*" declared Ben firmly.

"Not even a puff of smoke in the store cupboard?" asked Azzan hopefully.

"NO!" said Max. "But if you're good, we'll show you the costume after school," he added.

The gargoylz looked excited. "We will be," they chorused in delight.

Max and Ben couldn't believe their eyes when they trooped back into their classroom after lunch. The whole class was gathered around a mass of skirts, jackets, plastic leaves and a bright red cloak.

At the bottom, the tip of a long, furry brown tail poked out.

"The costumes!" yelled Max. "They've arrived!"

"I can see the wolf!" yelled Ben.

Max and Ben dived into the middle of the throng but Miss Bleet herded everyone into seats.

"I will be giving these out to the children who can wait quietly," she said, looking pointedly at the boys.

Max sat with his arms folded and lips squeezed tightly together and Ben put on his best innocent smile while their teacher handed out the costumes.

Soon all that was left was a furry brown outfit in four separate parts — two sets of trousers, a sort of long cape with a tail dangling down, and a wolf's head.

Miss Bleet held the pieces up. "And here's the wolf!"

Max and Ben gawped at it in horror and the rest of the class burst out laughing. The costume was soft and fluffy, with a sparkly pink collar

and a frilly bow between the ears.

"We can't wear that!" protested Ben above the sniggering. "Where are the fearsome teeth?"

"And the razor-sharp claws!" exclaimed Max.

"You'll just have to do the best you can with it," said Miss Bleet encouragingly. "I'm sure the collar and bow can be removed. That will make it more wolfish."

The boys took the costume and trailed gloomily back to their seats.

★ ★ ★

At home time Max and Ben waited until everyone else had gone before they dared to leave.

"Can't risk being seen with this horrible fluffy thing," declared Ben crossly as he mooched across the empty playground, the head and front legs of the wolf lolling over his arm. "It wasn't worth being good for."

"We're going to look really stupid in it," complained Max, carrying the back legs and the cape, with the wolf's tail dragging along behind.

Suddenly the legs and cape were pulled out of his grasp. They began to wiggle around at his feet. Then the front legs and head sprang out of Ben's arms. The bits of the wolf costume danced up and down the playground while lots of muffled gargoyle growling and giggling came from inside.

After a moment Toby's head popped out. "Do we look fierce?" he asked brightly.

"No one can look fierce in that thing!" sighed Max.

"It's not even as scary as Theo when he's being a tiger," added Ben.

"Nothing is as scary as me when I'm being a tiger!" said Theo proudly.

"But we're supposed to be really terrifying," said Max. "It'll ruin the whole play if we go on looking like a girl's cuddly toy!"

"I can make it terrifying," declared Barney shyly. "I'll sew some extra bits on it."

Everyone looked at him in astonishment.

"I know how to sew," Barney explained. "I've been watching the vicar's wife. You won't recognize that costume by the time I've finished."

"Dangling drainpipes!" said Azzan. "I thought you didn't like scary wolf costumes!"

"Whatever made you think that!" exclaimed Barney. "Leave it with me."

Max and Ben gave a yelp of delight.

"That would be awesome!" declared Ben. "Now, Barney, don't forget—"

"I know – fearsome teeth and razor-sharp clawz!" cried Barney.

"Absolutely!" said Max. "It's got to be—"

"The most scary wolf costume in the history of scary wolf costumes!" chorused all the gargoylz together.

3. Who's Afraid of the Big Bad Wolf?

It was Saturday, and Max and Ben sped along the pavement on their imaginary supersonic spy motorbike. They couldn't wait to find out what Barney had done to the wolf costume.

They zoomed past the locked school gates and whizzed into the churchyard.

"Any sign of them, Agent Neal?" asked Max, looking behind a gravestone.

"Not the tip of a dragony tail, Agent Black," said Ben, peering up at the church.

"RRRROOAAARRRR!"

The boys spun round to see a hideous

creature with vicious-looking claws loping
down the path towards them. It had lumps
of crinkled blue plastic all over its fur, one
of its ears was back-to-front, and sharp,
waxy-looking teeth sprouted from its
mouth at very odd angles. It skidded to a
halt, and glared at them.

"That's our wolf costume!" gasped Max.

"It *was* our costume," Ben corrected him. "It's fabulously gruesome now."

"Greetingz!" Toby's cheeky monkey face popped out of the wolf's mouth.

"Hope you like it," said Barney, appearing from the wolf's tummy. "Everyone helped but I put it all together."

"It's awesomely fantastic!" yelled Max.

"It took me ages to chop up the church candlez for the teeth," Toby told them proudly.

Theo clambered out. "I got the sticks for the clawz out of the vicar's garden," he said. "He won't need them. They were only holding up his sunflowerz. I had to break them all into bits."

Pop! Zack appeared in front of them. "Plasticky lumps! Plasticky lumps!" he said excitedly, pointing to the torn-up bits of blue supermarket bag. "I did those."

"We'll scare everyone with this!"

declared Ben. "It's just what we wanted. Thanks, gargoylz!"

"There is one little thing," said Max. "It's still a bit . . . well, fluffy."

"Leave that to me," said a gruff voice. The costume wriggled and jerked, and Azzan burst out onto the path. "I'll use my special power. Get back, everyone." He took a deep breath and blew a blast of flame at the wolf. There was a bright light and a smell of burning fur.

When the smoke had cleared, Max
and Ben peered at the wolf that lay in a
smoking heap on the path. The fur was
now black and singed and melted
together in places to form tufts.

"Cool!" sighed Ben. "That
is one horrible wolf!"

"Time to practise," said Max. "We can do it in the churchyard. No one's around."

"Can we help?" Theo pounced like a kitten on the costume's tail, his bottom quivering as he batted it with his paws.

"Of course," said Ben. "Me and Max have got to be really fierce. You lot could show us how to frighten everyone."

Suddenly they heard footsteps coming towards them. Barney squealed an alarm and the gargoylz scattered up the drainpipes and froze on the gutters with terrible grins on their faces. Max and Ben turned to see two old women in spotty overalls stomping flat-footedly up the path towards the church.

They had woolly hats rammed firmly
down on their grey perms and were
carrying baskets of flowers.

"It's all very well decorating the inside
of the church with these, Doris," one of
the women was saying grumpily, "but this
churchyard could do with a good clear-up
too."

"You're right, Aggie," replied the
other one in a whiny voice. "The
grass is far too long."

"And those gravestones
haven't had a polish
for years!" said
Aggie.

"The hinges
on the door are
creaky too,"
moaned Doris.
"Someone
should complain
to the vicar."

Aggie suddenly caught sight of Max and Ben. "And boys shouldn't be allowed in here. They make the place look even more untidy."

"Especially with their disgusting pets!" added Doris. She peered short-sightedly at the costume on the path. "It should be on a lead!" declared Aggie, shaking her basket at the boys.

At that moment there was a very rude noise and the air was filled with one of Barney's best bottom burps. Max and Ben backed away.

"And it stinks!" declared Doris, holding her nose.

The two old ladies scurried off into the

church. As soon
as the smell had
gone, the gargoylz
popped out of their
hiding places.

"Good one,
Barney!" chuckled
Max. "That got
rid of them."

"I didn't mean to," said Barney with a
shrug. "But they were rude about the wolf
costume and it made me cross."

"I've a good mind to burn their
baskets!" exclaimed Azzan, setting off after
them.

"Frazzled flowerz! Frazzled flowerz!"
chanted Zack, scurrying along behind him.

"There's no time for that!" exclaimed
Toby, flapping his wings urgently at his
gargoyle friends. "Right now we've got to
help Max and Ben rehearse."

"Toby's right," said Theo. "I must show

them how to be a fierce wolf – using my ferocious tiger power – otherwise the play will be a disaster!"

Max and Ben each pulled on their separate pairs of baggy wolf trousers. The trousers came up high above their waists and had straps that went over the boys' shoulders. Then Max bent forwards and grasped Ben round the waist. Ben put his head through the hole in the cape and settled it over his shoulders so that the fabric spread out to cover himself and Max. It draped over them to make the main body of the wolf.

"I can only see the ground from here!" came Max's muffled voice from the back.

"Don't worry," Ben told him cheerfully as he pulled the wolf's head on. "I've got a good view through the mouth. Just follow my lead. We'll try a bit of walking first. That shouldn't be too difficult."

He set off along the path.

Max suddenly felt himself being pulled forward. He tripped on his own paw, lost his balance, and the wolf collapsed in a heap. The boys could hear gales of gargoyle giggling.

"Give us a bit of warning next time," groaned Max as he and Ben untangled themselves and struggled to their feet.

"Left foot first. Here we go!" said Ben firmly.

After colliding with a stone angel, falling over three gravestones and getting tangled up in a gorse bush, the wolf eventually learned to walk, run and even jump.

"Success, Agent Black!" shouted its front half.

"Success, Agent Neal!" shouted its back half. "But I'm getting a bit hot," Max added, sticking his head out from under the side of the cape.

"It's time for your lesson in being fierce," Theo told them. "Don't be alarmed, but I'm going to turn into a tiger first, so that I can be really ferocious."

The other gargolyz lined up on the wall to watch as the determined little gargoyle let out a **miaow** and began to wriggle. His stone began to turn into soft tabby fur.

"Poor old Theo," Ben whispered over his shoulder to Max. "He can still only manage to change into a little kitten. He's very cute, but not very scary."

"Don't forget he's only a young gargoyle," Max reminded him. "Give him another four hundred and twelve years and he might get the hang of becoming a tiger."

"Now I'm going to show you how to pounce," announced Theo the kitten grandly. He launched himself at the wolf, bounced off its nose and landed on his back in a bush.

The gargoylz applauded loudly and Theo took several bows.

"Your turn," Theo told the wolf as he hopped up onto the wall to join his friends.

"I don't think we'll be as fierce as you," said Ben, "but we'll do our best. Ready, Agent Black?"

"Ready, Agent Neal," replied Max, disappearing back inside the wolf.

"This is awesome," came Ben's voice. "There are strings in here to make the mouth move."

He made the big bad wolf open its huge, toothy mouth even wider. "One . . . two . . . three . . . **ROARRRRRRRR!**" he yelled as he and Max attempted to make the wolf pounce like Theo.

The gargoylz took one look at the wild, bloodshot eyes and pointed teeth lurching towards them, and fled. Zack vanished with a **pop**! Barney, Azzan and Theo dived into the long grass, and Toby was

so terrified he scampered twice round the
churchyard and froze on a pillar by the
church porch.

Theo's nose poked out of the grass. "Well done, boyz," he said with a shaky grin. "I'm glad my scaring lesson worked."

"It certainly did!" laughed Ben, taking off the wolf's head. "It frightened you lot."

"I wish I'd seen that!" said the back end of the wolf, and Max's head emerged.

"We weren't frightened," said Barney, creeping nervously from his hiding place.

"We were just . . . stretching our legz," insisted Azzan as he scampered back along the path.

"Keeping fit! Keeping fit!" declared Zack, appearing with a **pop!** and pretending to do some running on the spot.

"Now we need to find some humans to scare," said Ben, putting the wolf's head on again, ready for action. "Shame Lucinda and her friends aren't around."

Suddenly he noticed that Toby was still

frozen by the porch, wings outstretched and mouth wide open.

"Toby!" he called. "It's OK – you can come back now."

Then they all heard the sound of flat feet, and two dumpy figures came out of the church.

Max poked out his head and put his spy radar on red alert: spotty overalls, woolly hats, whingeing voices. He knew what that meant. It was Enemy Agents Doris and Aggie, codename: Demon Flower Arrangers.

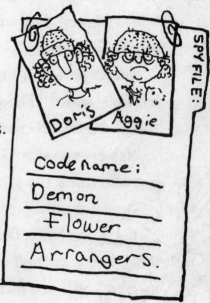

Doris

Aggie

SPY FILE:

Code name:
Demon
Flower
Arrangers.

"And there's another thing I don't like about this place . . ." Doris was saying as she came into view. "Those gargoyles are the ugliest creatures

I've ever seen!"

Now the boys knew why Toby had frozen. Quick as a flash the rest of the gargoylz ducked down behind a tombstone. The front of the wolf followed, dragging the back end after it.

"You're quite right, Doris," Max heard Aggie agree. "This one by the door is the worst of the lot!"

Azzan let out a furious – and rather smoky – snort. "They're talking about Toby!" he hissed crossly.

"It's ever so dirty," grumbled Doris. "I really think the vicar should give them all a scrub."

Max, Ben and the gargoylz peeped over the gravestone to see that Doris had whipped out a lacy pink hankie. To their horror, she gave it a big lick and then began to rub it over Toby's nose!

Toby stayed frozen, his eyes wide with
disgust.

"I don't think this one's
been cleaned for years,"
puffed Doris as she
poked the hankie
into one of Toby's
ears and twiddled
it around. "The
grime just won't
come off. It's going
to take me ages."

"Whoever heard of a clean gargoyle?"
hissed Azzan. "We've got to stop them!"

"We should chase them off!" insisted
Zack.

"We can't do that," said Barney, his
spines quivering nervously. "We'll be seen."

"But *we* can!" declared Max. "Time
for a new secret plan, Agent Neal –
Secret Plan: Save Toby from Horrible
Old Biddies."

"Brilliant, Agent Black," exclaimed Ben. "It'll be good scaring practice too."

He rammed on the wolf's head and Max disappeared inside its tummy. Keeping out of sight, the wolf crept between the grasses and gravestones towards the old ladies. At last Max felt Ben stop.

"Old biddy target straight ahead," Ben whispered. "When I growl, we charge."

Doris was now red in the face with the effort of rubbing at Toby's stone. "It's no good," she said at last. "I can't shift this muck."

Aggie plunged a hand into her bag. "Try using this," she said, handing Doris a huge, prickly nailbrush. "I find one of these is always useful in an emergency."

"I'll give its teeth a good scrub," declared Doris, rolling up her sleeves. "They're horrible."

"**GRRRRRRR!**" growled Ben in his
most ferocious voice. And then he and
Max leaped forward.

Aggie let out an ear-piercing shriek
and Doris dropped the brush in fright. As
Max and Ben charged at them in the wolf
costume, the two old women took to their
heels. They scuttled down the path and out
of the churchyard. Soon they were out of
sight.

"*I'll huff and I'll puff and I'll—*" Ben
yelled menacingly after them.

"Wrong story!" Max hissed.

"Who cares?" answered Ben, pulling off
his wolf's head. "We got rid of them!"

The boys clambered out of the costume
and high-fived. Toby flew over to join
them, spitting crossly and wiping his face
with his wing. The other gargoylz gathered
round him.

"Spluttering gutterz, that was terrible!" he puffed.

Theo began to chuckle. "But you did look funny with a pink hankie in your ear," he spluttered.

"He didn't look funny," said Azzan loyally. "He just looked a bit like a flower."

"Don't want to look like a flower," huffed Toby.

"It's OK," Barney reassured him. "They didn't manage to clean any of your stone."

"Dirty and grimy! Dirty and grimy!" called Zack.

Toby grinned with relief. "I'd never have been able to show my face on the church roof if they'd *cleaned* me! Thank you for rescuing me, boyz."

"Don't thank us," said Ben. "Thank the wolf costume."

"Ben's right," said Max, grinning. "The wolf was definitely the star of the show!"

4. Show Time!

"I'm so excited," said Ben. "I feel like I've got fizzy lemonade bubbling around in my tummy."

"I've got rampaging rhinos in mine!" said Max.

It was the night of the play and Max and Ben were whizzing through the playground on their imaginary superspy jet-skis. They darted through the crowds of arriving parents and zoomed over to the churchyard wall.

"Gargoylz," whispered Ben. "Are you there?"

Five excited heads popped up from behind a nearby gravestone.

"Is it time for the show?" asked Toby, flying over to join the boys.

Max nodded. "Very soon. You'll be watching, won't you?"

"We'll be there," purred Theo.

"We can't wait," added Azzan.

"Wolvz and axes! Wolvz and axes!"

chanted Zack as he bounded around the churchyard.

"You'll have to keep out of sight," warned Ben. "You don't want humans to see you."

"Don't worry," said Barney. "You won't even know we're there."

Max and Ben sped back into school and got the singed and gruesome wolf costume out of the classroom store cupboard. They'd hidden it there so no one would see it before the big night.

"The gargoylz have done a wonderful job," said Max. "Miss True's going to be dead impressed."

"We'll be the star of the show," agreed Ben. He picked up his wolf trousers and tucked the head under his arm. "Let's wait in the wings."

Miss True took one look at the costume and nearly dropped her cup of tea. "You certainly have made some changes," she gasped.

"Don't you like it?" asked Max, worried.

"It's great." Miss True smiled as she saw the wonky ear and blackened fur. "You've made it very . . . fierce." She checked her watch. "Now go

and put the costume on — and no scaring
the girls!"

In great excitement the boys got into
their suit. Ben slipped the ferocious head
on. "I can see Tiffany," he whispered over
his shoulder. "We should go and tell her
to break a leg. That's how actors
wish each other good luck.
It won't be our fault if we
accidentally scare her
at the same time."

They sidled up to
Tiffany, who was
in her grandma's
nightdress costume.

"**Grrrr!**" roared
Ben. "Break a leg!"

Tiffany shrieked
and ran away.

"Low five, Agent
Neal," called Max, slapping
his friend on the back.

"Places, everyone," called Miss True. "Show starts in two minutes."

Ben crept over to the curtain, pulled it back a little and peered out of the wolf's mouth. "There are loads of people out there," he reported. "Your mum's sitting right at the front. I can just see Mrs Hogsbum and . . . no . . . I can't see the gargoylz. They must have found a really good hiding place."

"Ben! Max!" called Miss True. "Get back here!"

The Oldacre School orchestra struck up a wobbly tune and the curtain swished open. Lucinda tripped onto the stage in her Red Riding Hood costume. She sang a sickly song in the spotlight while the squirrels, flowers and trees danced around her, yodelling the chorus. Then she pirouetted to the front.

"I'm skipping off to Dingly Dell," she lisped in a sugary tone, "to see my gran.

She's not been well. I've got some cookies for her tea. She'll perk right up when she sees me."

"Lucinda's even more yucky than in rehearsals!" Max hissed up at Ben.

"Pity we can't just gobble *her* up," Ben hissed back.

"I promised Mum I wouldn't stray," Lucinda went on, tossing her golden ringlets under her bright red hood. "But see those flowers along the way ..."

As she left the safety of the path, the Max-and-Ben wolf lurched out from the wings and tiptoed across the wooden stage towards her with an evil snigger.

"Hello, little girl!" Ben growled sweetly, pulling on the strings to make the mouth move as if the wolf was talking. "What's in your basket?"

"Awesome, Agent Neal!" whispered Max from somewhere near Ben's bottom. "Word perfect."

"Treats for my sick grandmama," trilled Lucinda. "Cookies, cakes and— **Aaargh!** A *monkey*!" She dropped the basket on the stage and gawped in horror at it. "There," she wailed, pointing at the basket. "Eating the goodies!"

"They're not the proper words," muttered Max. "They don't rhyme."

Ben peered into the basket. A cheeky stone face covered in crumbs was grinning up at him.

"It's Toby!" he hissed. "He mustn't be seen!" He whipped round to hide the basket from the audience, swinging the back end of the wolf about so fast that Max fell over with his tail tangled round his legs. The audience thought it was part of the play and roared with laughter. As Max struggled to his feet, Ben shot a hand out from under the front of the cape, scooped Toby up by the tail and pulled him inside.

Toby scrambled into the front of Max's wolf trousers and grinned up at him, safely hidden by the wolf cape that covered them.

"Dangling drainpipes!" he shouted in delight. "My plan worked. I'm in the play!"

Meanwhile Lucinda was still gawping at the basket like a goldfish. The play had ground to a halt. Ben realized he would have to give her the basket back – but he couldn't pick it up with his hand; wolves

didn't have hands. Instead he wobbled desperately on one leg and hooked the basket up with his foot/paw.

"Here you are, little girl," he snarled, pushing the basket into Lucinda's trembling hands.

Holding the basket at arm's length as if it might bite her, Lucinda stuttered through her next lines and ran from the stage.

"I'm going to get to Grandma's house before her," declared the Max-Ben-and-now-Toby wolf to the audience. And the fierce creature lolloped off in the opposite direction.

The delighted audience hissed and booed
loudly as it went.

"This is fun," whispered
Toby as they jogged along.

"Just keep still!" Max
told him firmly. "No
wriggling."

The next scene
showed Red Riding
Hood slowly making
her way to Grandma's
cottage. Lucinda skipped
and pranced across the
front of the stage, stopping
to smell flowers as she went.
Meanwhile the wolf charged through the
cardboard bushes and dancing trees at the
back to get to Grandma's house first.

Ben was just turning towards the
audience to give a horrible growly laugh
when something tugged at one of Max's
furry feet.

"Can I be in the play?" It was Barney, hiding behind a brightly painted fern.

"You shouldn't be here!" exclaimed Max in horror.

He stuck out a hand, snatched up Barney and tucked him firmly into the top of his trousers before galloping off behind Ben towards the cottage.

"Greetingz!" chirped Toby as the shy little gargoyle settled himself down next to him.

"I hope the others aren't up to anything," Max called to Ben. "There's not much room left back here."

The dancing trees pranced off the stage and a sheet of flowery wallpaper unrolled at the back. Two squirrels (Barry Price and Duncan) pushed a bed into the middle of the stage and scampered off.

Tiffany came hobbling on as Grandma.

"Oh, dearie me," she said in a croaky voice. "I have the flu. Here comes a sneeze ... **Waa-haa-tish-ooooo!**"

The Max-Ben-Toby-and-now-Barney wolf knocked at the door.

"Who comes to call on poor old me?" called Tiffany.

"It's Red Riding Hood, I've brought your tea," replied the wolf in a high-pitched squeak.

Tiffany pretended to open a door and the wolf bounded onto the stage.

"Whoooaaaa!" called Barney, gripping tightly to Max's knee. "Slow down!"

"**Shhhh!**" hissed Max. As the wolf opened its slavering jaws to gobble up Grandma, the lights dimmed and drums rolled dramatically. In the darkness Tiffany was lowered down through a trapdoor in the stage.

100

When the lights came up again, everyone gasped – the old lady was nowhere to be seen. Ben let out a loud burp and rubbed his tummy – just to show that the wolf had enjoyed his Grandma dinner.

The trapdoor was slowly rising back into place now, but to Ben's alarm, it wasn't empty. **Pop!** Zack's head appeared from the darkness below. Of course Ben knew what he had to do. Faster than rain down a spout, he snatched up Zack and stuffed him under the costume on top of Max's back. Now the wolf had a hump like a camel.

"Greetingz!" declared Toby, giving Zack a thumbs-up.

"We're in the play! We're in the play!" yelled Zack, squirming with excitement and peeping down at Toby from Max's back.

"**Shhhh!**" said Max.

"**ROOOAAARRR!**" yelled Ben, to drown them all out. "Now I'll pretend to be old Grandma and lie in wait for Little Red Riding Hood."

The audience laughed and booed, and the Max-Ben-Toby-Barney-and-now-Zack wolf took a quick bow before scampering off behind a screen.

Miss True was waiting for the boys. She gave the wolf's lumpy shape a puzzled glance as she pulled a nightdress over the costume and stuck a nightcap on top of the furry wolf's ears.

Then the wolf ran on stage again and
made for the bed.

Max's bit of the wolf was completely
under the covers for this part of the play.
As he scrambled into the bed and began
to snuggle down, he heard a low miaow
of protest. There was something already in
the bed and it was in the way. Carefully he
peeked out of the costume.

"Theo!" he gasped.

The little gargoyle was curled up under
the sheets, his stripy tail wrapped around
him.

"I wanted to be in the play," whispered Theo. "And this bed's cosy. Just right for a catnap."

"Well, you can't stay here," said Max grimly. Under cover of the sheets, he scooped him up and squeezed him into the wolf costume between Toby and Barney.

"Greetingz!" said Toby, making room for him.

"Cosy in here too," purred Theo, waving up at Zack.

"Crowded, you mean," grumbled Max. It was hard to get comfortable with his suit full of gargoylz.

"Keep still," Ben hissed from the front end. "I've got lines coming up. I mustn't get them wrong."

"What big eyes you've got, Grandma," came Lucinda's voice.

"I've got big eyez," Theo told Max. "I could play that part."

"All the butter ... I mean, better ... to see you with," Ben growled at Lucinda. Then, "Quiet in there," he muttered. "You're putting me off."

"What big ears you've got!" Lucinda went on.

"All the better to—"

"What a rude girl!" shouted Toby. "My earz aren't that big."

"**Shhhh!**" Max gave him a nudge and nearly fell out of the bed.

"What big teeth you've got, Grandma," said Red Riding Hood.

"All the better to eat you with!" roared the Max-Ben-Toby-Barney-Zack-and-now-Theo wolf, leaping out of the bed.

"Oh, no, you don't, you big bad wolf!" Gavin the woodcutter cried, striding onto the stage. He was carrying a sack and a big axe. He threw the sack to the floor and raised the axe over his head.

This was Ben's favourite bit of the play – the fight scene. He kicked out with his feet as if trying to maul Gavin with his claws. Then he pulled hard on the strings inside his costume, making the mouth open and close, just as if the wolf was snapping at its prey.

"**GRRRRR!**" he roared, getting ready to pounce. Max wiggled his bottom to make the wolf's tail swish menacingly. Then he

saw something on the stage near his feet.
Two dragony wings were sticking out of
the woodcutter's sack.

"Oh, no," he whispered urgently to Ben.
"Azzan's in the sack!"

Thinking quickly, Ben bent down to
make it look as if the wolf was trying to
tear the sack to pieces with its teeth. Then
he reached out one hand and pulled the
fire-breathing gargoyle inside the costume.

"Greetingz!" said Toby as Azzan scrambled in amongst his gargoyle friends, trying to find a place to perch.

Gavin gawped as the wolf bulged all over.

At last Azzan made his way up Ben's back to his shoulder and held onto his ear. He peered out of the wolf's mouth. "I can see everything," he called down to his friends.

"Humanz and lights and axes – although it's a bit fluffy in here."

"**RROOOAARRRR!**" The Max-Ben-Toby-Barney-Zack-Theo-and-now-Azzan wolf lumbered towards Gavin. The woodcutter waited patiently for the wolf to reach him.

"You shouldn't eat so many thistles, gargoylz," grumbled Max. "You're heavy!"

He looked down to make sure that the wolf was now standing on the trapdoor in the stage, ready for its last big moment. When Gavin gave the cue, the wolf would be lowered under the stage to swap places with Tiffany. Then, as the trapdoor went back up, it would look as if Grandma had been freed from the wolf's stomach. It had gone very well in rehearsal. The dinner ladies had been watching and they'd all gasped in amazement; Mrs Simmer, the head cook, had fanned them with her ladle.

"You've eaten your last grandma!" yelled Gavin, and he swiped the air with his plastic axe.

Those were the words for the transformation. Max heard the whir of the trapdoor and felt himself starting to descend into the dark.

"I've got fluff up my nose," remarked Azzan suddenly, and then, with a huge sneeze, he let out a great burst of fire. It shot from the wolf's mouth in a jet. Gavin jumped back just in time to save his eyebrows.

"Ooh!" gasped the audience, clapping wildly at the wonderful special effect.

The wolf disappeared and Tiffany popped up in its place.

Under the stage, Ben threw off the wolf's head. His hair was smoking slightly but he was grinning broadly. "Did you hear that applause?" he cried happily. "They loved us!"

"Brilliant fire, Azzan," agreed Max. "Just what we needed to make a dramatic exit."

"I like being a wolf," miaowed Theo, cleaning his paws. "Though not as much as being a tiger, of course."

They heard the curtains swish closed and the audience burst into loud applause again.

"Places, everyone," called Miss True. "Time to take your bows."

When the Max-Ben-Toby-Barney-Zack-Theo-and-Azzan wolf

lumbered onto the stage, the audience cheered and stamped their feet.

"They'll have the roof off," shouted Ben over the clamour as he and Max took their fifteenth bow and nearly fell over with the weight of the gargoylz.

The applause finally died down, and Max and Ben trotted off to the toilets to set the gargoylz free.

"Spluttering gutterz!" declared Toby as they all burst out of the wolf's tummy. "I haven't had so much fun since we put custard in the vicar's bed!"

"When's the next play?" demanded Azzan.

"Next year," Max told them. "Why?"

"Because we want to be in it!" shouted the gargoylz.

Gargoylz Fact File

Full name: Tobias the Third
Known as: Toby
Special Power: Flying
Likes: All kinds of pranks and mischief – especially playing jokes on the vicar
Dislikes: Mrs Hogsbottom, garden gnomes

Full name: Barnabas
Known as: Barney
Special Power: Making big stinks!
Likes: Cookiez
Dislikes: Being surprised by humanz

Full name: Eli
Special Power: Turning into a grass snake
Likes: Sssports Day, Sssslithering
Dislikes: Ssscary ssstories

Full name: Bartholomew

Known as: Bart

Special Power: Burping spiders

Likes: Being grumpy

Dislikes: Being told to cheer up

Full name: Theophilus

Known as: Theo

Special Power: Turning into a ferocious tiger (well, tabby kitten!)

Likes: Sunny spots and cosy places

Dislikes: Rain

Full name: Zackary

Known as: Zack

Special Power: Making himself invisible to humanz

Likes: Bouncing around, eating bramblz, thistlz, and anything with pricklz!

Dislikes: Keeping still

Full name: Ira
Special Power: Making it rain
Likes: Making humans walk the plank
Dislikes: Being bored

Name: Azzan
Special Power: Breathing fire
Likes: Surprises
Dislikes: Smoke going up his nose and making him sneeze

Name: Cyrus
Special Power: Sings lullabies to send humanz to sleep
Likes: Fun days out
Dislikes: Snoring